Roger Gets Carried Away

By Barbara Todd

Art by Rogé

ANNICK PRESS

Toronto • New York • Vancouver

Roger, who was secretly known as Captain Kaboodle, could imagine almost anything.

When his mother said something was growing under his bed and she couldn't imagine where it came from, Captain Kaboodle could.

"It's

Astro Blob!"

Luckily, some helpful dinosaurs bounced the Blob into another galaxy.

"Honestly, Roger!" said his mother. "You get so carried away. Now hurry up or we'll be late." It was time to go to the eye doctor.

Eye doctor? "YIIIIIKeS!" yelped Roger. "GLASSeS!"

Even Roger couldn't imagine that.

When they got home, Roger stuck his glasses in his pocket.

"They're sturdy and sensible," insisted his mother.

"But I'm Captain Kaboodle!" cried Roger. "I don't need glasses. I've got perfect X-ray vision!"

That night, Roger worked on his latest invention –
the BLASTO-TRAVELER.

"I hope this works," he said. "Captain Kaboodle –
Space Ranger!"

Roger pushed the red button and …

ZAP!

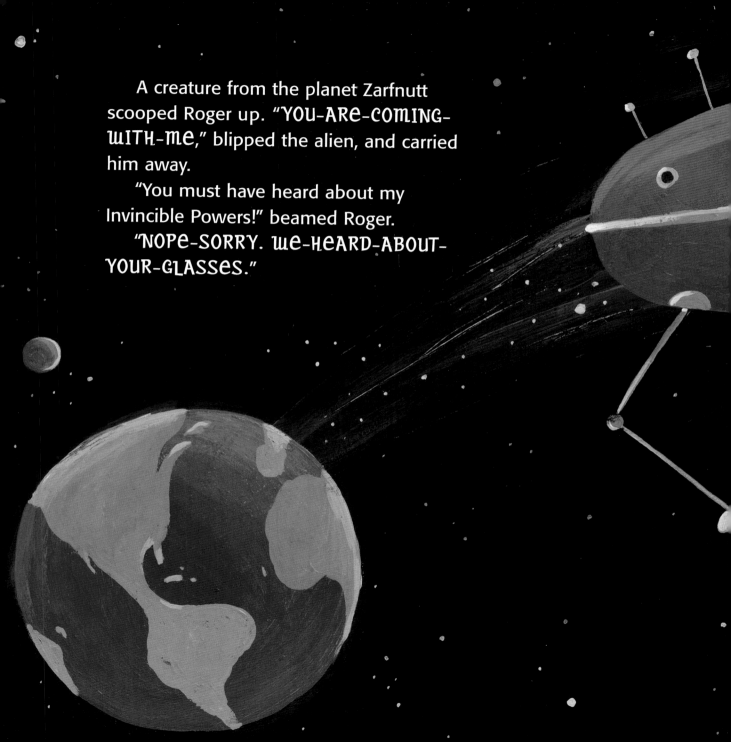

A creature from the planet Zarfnutt scooped Roger up. "YOU-ARE-COMING-WITH-ME," blipped the alien, and carried him away.

"You must have heard about my Invincible Powers!" beamed Roger.

"NOPE-SORRY. WE-HEARD-ABOUT-YOUR-GLASSES."

"CAPTAIN KABOODLE DOESN'T NEED GLASSES!!!"

howled Roger. It echoed across the galaxy.

When the spaceship landed, the Zarfnutts were waiting. "WE-NEED-GLASSES."

"You need lots of glasses," said Roger. "You should go to the eye doctor."

"CAPTAIN-KABOODLE, EYE-DOCTOR!" answered the aliens. "YOU'VE-GOT-STURDY-SENSIBLE-GLASSES."

"But I don't NEED them!" wailed Roger.

The Zarfnutts blinked their bug-eyed alien eyes and sniffled.

The eye Doctor is in

"Oh, all right," said Roger. "Who's first? Close your left eyes and read this line."

"GRUNGLE-ZOG-BURP!" bleeped an alien.

"You need glasses," said Roger. "Here! Take mine."

The alien tried them on. They didn't fit, so he ate them.

CRUNCH!

"Yippee!" hooted Roger. "They'll be mashed into a million pieces!"

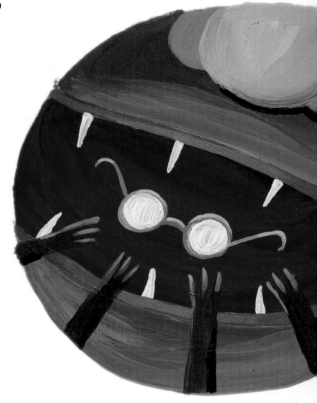

"BLURRRRRRP!"

"Aww, nuts!" groaned Roger. He tried every creature on Zarfnutt, but his sturdy, sensible glasses just didn't fit any of them.

"**MORE-GLASSES**," burbled the aliens.
They pointed to a map. "**GALAXY-GLASSES-ON-PLANET-ZORKLE**."

BLASTO-TRAVELER

"This is a job for Captain Kaboodle!"
cried Roger. He rocketed into space.
Roger tried to follow the map, but he wasn't wearing his glasses.

SPLATTT!!!

"It's a humongous rubber-bellied Astro Blob!"
Roger pushed the Anti-Sticky button on
his BLASTO-TRAVELER.
"Captain Kaboodle to the rescue!"

SPLOOSH!

They bounced back into the galaxy.
"WE-ARE-LOST," squonked the alien.
"Impossible!" cried Roger. "Captain
Kaboodle has BLORPP-Radar!"

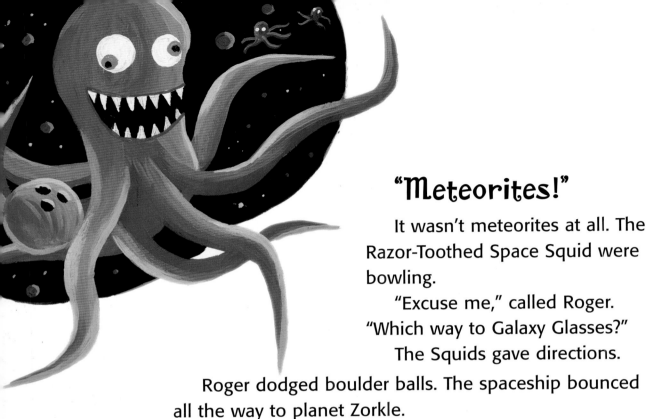

"**Meteorites!**"

It wasn't meteorites at all. The Razor-Toothed Space Squid were bowling.

"Excuse me," called Roger. "Which way to Galaxy Glasses?"

The Squids gave directions.

Roger dodged boulder balls. The spaceship bounced all the way to planet Zorkle.

"**MAYBE-YOU-NEED-GLASSES,**" the alien glurped.

"I DON'T NEED GLASSES!" yelped Roger.

He was looking for a place to land, when –

PLUNK!

"We've been Spacenapped by a One-Eyed Humbug!"
The Humbug smacked his rubbery lips.

"DON'T EAT US!" Roger pleaded.

But the one-eyed, no-eared Humbug wasn't listening.

"WE-WILL-BE-SQUOOSHED-TO-SMITHEREENS!" blubbered the Zarfnutt alien.

"Never fear!" cried Roger. "Captain Kaboodle saves the day!" He put on his sturdy, sensible glasses. "You're not going to like this."

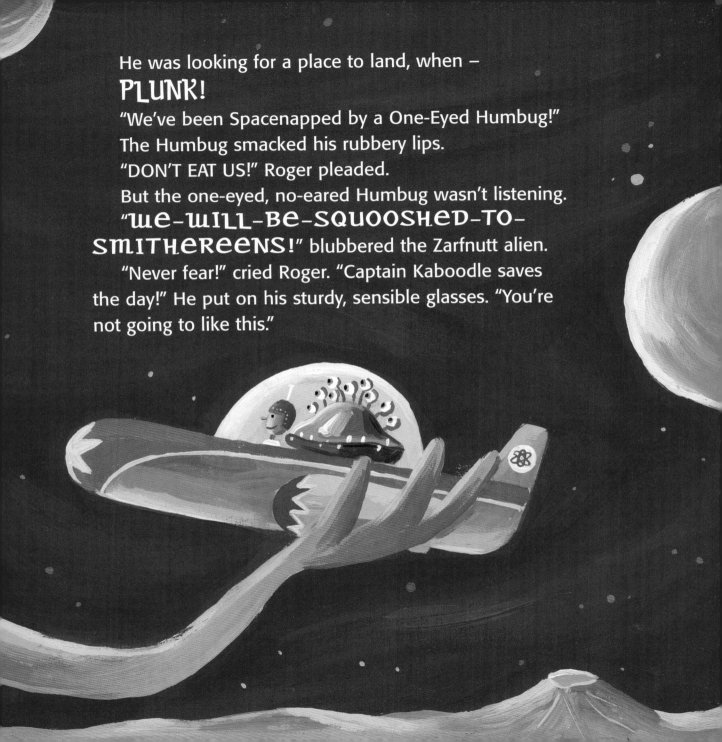

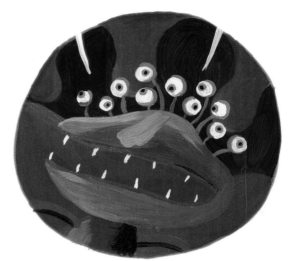

CRUNCH

'BLURRRRRRP!

The Humbug swallowed Roger for supper, then he licked his chops and gulped the alien for dessert.

CRUNCH. But even one-eyed monsters won't eat sturdy, sensible glasses.

"Blurrrrrp!"

"It worked!" cried Roger. He wiped off the slime and put his glasses back on.

"WOW!"
Roger had never imagined this before.
He could see everything.

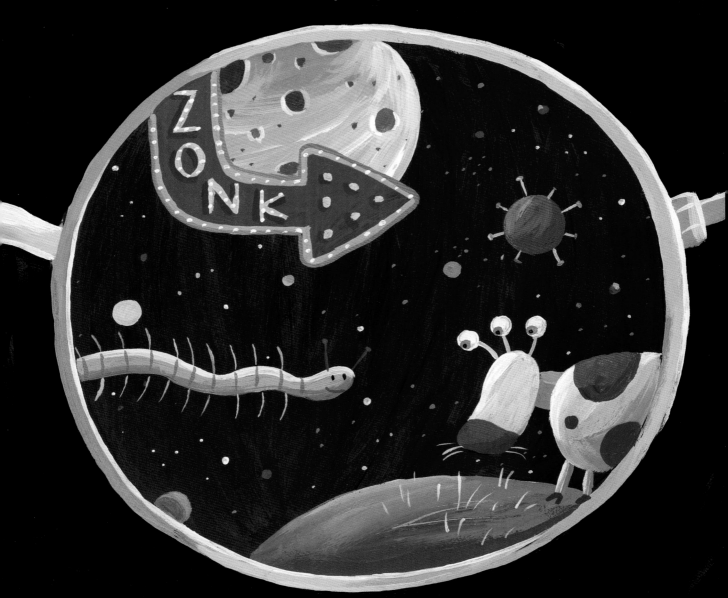

"There's the Galaxy Glasses Shop!" exclaimed Roger. "He's captured all the glasses!"

But the Humbug didn't have *all* the glasses. He snatched Roger's sturdy, sensible pair.

"HEY!" hollered Roger.

I NEED MY GLASSES!

"BUT I LOVE GLASSES!" wibbled the Humbug.

"Perfect!" said Roger. "You can be the new eye doctor!"

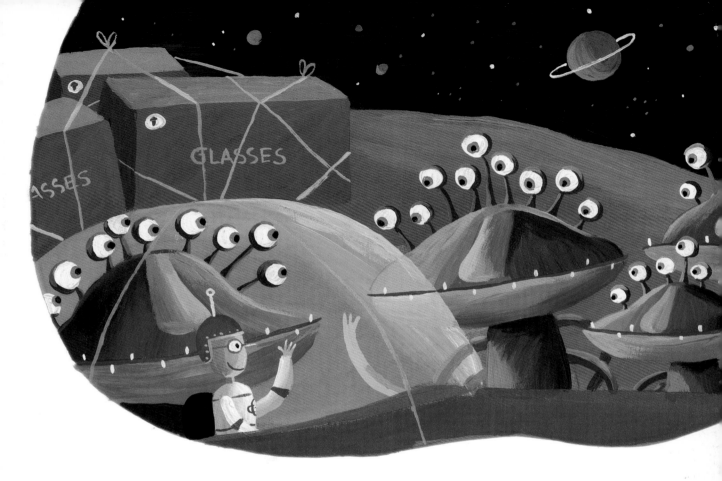

Roger went shopping at Galaxy Glasses.

"I need a billion pairs of Bug-Eyed Expandable Alien Spectacles, please."

When they returned, the Zarfnutts greeted them. "NOTHING-IS-IMPOSSIBLE-FOR-CAPTAIN-KABOODLE!"

Roger waved. He set the BLASTO-TRAVELER for HOME.
"Captain Kaboodle – Earthling!"
He pushed the green button and …

ZAP!

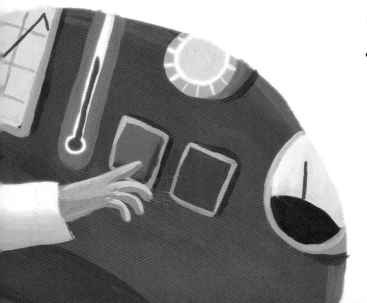

Roger's mother put supper on the table. Roger could see it perfectly. It looked green and furry and suspiciously like an alien.

"Astro Blob returns!"

He'd had enough aliens for one day. Roger set the dial to DINOSAURS.

"Captain Kaboodle – Jungle Explorer!"

"Goodness, Roger!" his mother sighed.

"I can't imagine how you get so carried away!"

But Roger could imagine it perfectly.

He pushed the red button and …

ZAP!

We acknowledge the support of the Canada Council for the Arts, the Ontario Arts Council, and the Government of Canada through the Book Publishing Industry Develop-ment Program (BPIDP) for our publishing activities.

Cataloging in Publication

Todd, Barbara, 1961-
Roger gets carried away / by Barbara Todd ; art by Rogé.

ISBN 1-55037-899-6 (bound).—ISBN 1-55037-898-8 (pbk.)

I. Rogé, 1972- II. Title.

PS8589.O59R63 2005   jC813'.6   C2004-904913-5

The art in this book was rendered in acrylic.
The text was typeset in Formata and Baileywick JF-Festive.

Distributed in Canada by:
Firefly Books Ltd.
66 Leek Crescent
Richmond Hill, ON
L4B 1H1

Published in the U.S.A. by Annick Press (U.S.) Ltd.
Distributed in the U.S.A. by:
Firefly Books (U.S.) Inc.
P.O. Box 1338
Ellicott Station
Buffalo, NY 14205

Printed in China.

Visit us at: www.annickpress.com

For Michael, Ben, Hannah and Keith
—B.T.

Pour Marilou
—R.G.